A FOREVER
Christmas

A FOREVER
Christmas

A BLACK FAMILY HOLIDAY STORY

SANDI LYNN

DEDICATION

A Forever Christmas was inspired by my mom and sister over dinner one Saturday night at P.F. Changs.

This book is dedicated to Joyce and Sue.

CHAPTER ONE

Ellery

After Connor and I brought the kids home from the toy store, we made them some hot chocolate and told them that after they drank it, it was time for bed. Tomorrow, we were going look for a Christmas tree. Connor helped me make the hot chocolate and then he went into his office to do some work.

"Now be very careful with your hot chocolate. It's very hot and I don't want you burning yourself."

"I won't, Mommy. I'm a big girl. I'm seven." Julia smiled.

"I'm a big boy," Collin said.

"No, you're not. You're only five. You're still a baby."

"AM NOT!" he began to scream.

I closed my eyes and took a deep breath. "Julia, don't call your brother a baby and Collin stop screaming."

Connor walked back into the kitchen. "What's going on in here?"

"Julia called me a baby."

"Well, he is." She smirked at Connor.

"Daddy!" Collin screamed.

I looked at Connor and put my hand on his chest. "Thank you for coming back in here to take care of them. I'm going to take a nice hot bubble bath," I said as I kissed his lips.

"But—"

"No buts, baby. I'll help you tuck the children in bed when I'm done."

I walked upstairs and started my bath. I loved my children more than life itself, but there were some days where I just let Connor deal with the arguing. Not to say that he was any better at controlling them. Julia had him wrapped around her finger. All she had to do was smile at him and he melted. After getting undressed, I climbed into the bubbly tub and sighed. It wasn't too long after when there was a light knock on the bathroom door.

"Mommy, can I come in for a minute?"

Well, that didn't last long. "Sure, Julia. You can come in."

She walked in, holding up two pairs of pajamas. "I'm not sure which one I should wear tonight. What do you think, Mommy?"

"Where's Daddy, Julia?"

"He's helping Collin get into his pajamas. Please don't change the subject."

My seven-year-old little girl was nothing short of a diva and I blamed Mason and Connor. They'd both deny it, but the way they spoiled her was unreal.

"I like the pink pair with the pretty white lace."

"Why?" she asked. "Don't you like the purple ones?"

"There you are, Julia," Connor said as he walked into the bathroom.

"Daddy, which ones do you like the best?"

He bent down so he was at her level. "I like them both. I think you look beautiful in any one you wear, and considering you just wore the purple ones this week, why don't you wear the pink ones?"

"Thank you, Daddy," she said as hugged him and kissed him on the cheek.

I looked at Connor and rolled my eyes.

"What?" he asked as he knelt down in front of the tub, picked up my loofah sponge, and started rubbing it in circles across my arm.

"Nothing. You're the apple of her eye."

"I know and I love it." He smiled. "You know what else I love?"

"What?" I asked.

"The thought of making love to you after the kids are asleep." He smiled as his hand traveled under the water and he slipped his fingers inside of me.

I moaned and bit down on my bottom lip until Julia came running back into the bathroom.

"Daddy, why is your hand in Mommy's bath water?"

He froze and stared at me for the answer. "My hand was cold and I was warming it up," he said.

I almost busted into laughter. "That's the best you can come up with?" I whispered.

"Oh. You're weird, Daddy. Come on; tuck me in to bed and read me a story."

"Okay, princess. Go get in bed and I'll be there in a minute."

"You better go, Daddy, before your little princess questions you some more." I smiled.

"Very funny, Elle. You better hurry and get out of this tub. I have all-night plans for you and that beautiful body of yours." He winked as he dried off his hand, leaving me aroused.

He left the bathroom and I couldn't be in more awe of him.

I slipped on my robe and walked into Collin's room. He was sound asleep and he looked like such an angel. I picked up his clothes off the floor and threw them in the hamper, and then I leaned over and kissed his head goodnight. After I walked out of his room, I went across the hall to Julia's, where I stood in the doorway and listened to Connor read her a princess story.

"So the little princess loved her daddy so much that she vowed never to get married and lived with her parents forever."

I shook my head and Julia giggled. "It doesn't say that, Daddy."

Connor set the book down and reached over and tickled her. "It should say that." He laughed.

I walked in and kissed Julia good night. "Good night, my sweet baby girl." I smiled.

"Good night, Mommy. Good night, Daddy."

"Night, princess. I love you."

"I love you both too."

Connor placed his hand on the small of my back and, as soon as he shut Julia's door, he chased me down the hall and into our bedroom. He fulfilled his promise and his plans involving my body all night long.

CHAPTER TWO

Connor

After my shower, I went down to the kitchen for some breakfast. The aroma of pumpkin spice pancakes filled the air.

"Good morning," I said as I walked over to Collin's and Julia's seats and kissed their heads.

"Morning, Dad," Collin replied.

"Good morning, my handsome daddy." Julia smiled.

I looked at Ellery and she rolled her eyes. She poured me a cup of coffee and handed it to me as I placed my arm around her waist.

"I hope you're not too sore from last night," I whispered.

"Why would Mommy be sore?" Julia asked.

Ellery shot me a look, and I shook my head. "Your turn," I mouthed as I walked away.

"I did some exercises last night before bed, Julia."

"What kind of exercises?" she asked.

"Leg exercises. Stretches, lunges, squats," I replied.

I was getting hard listening to her so I walked over and pressed myself against her. "You need to stop talking like that."

A few moments later, Mason walked into the kitchen. "Good morning, my happy little family. It smells delicious in here!"

"Mommy's sore from all the exercises she did last night before bed," Julia said.

Mason looked at me and rolled his eyes. "I bet she is."

Ellery gave Mason her cute smile and handed him a plate of pancakes.

"What are you doing here on a Saturday?" I asked.

"I'm going with your family to pick out a Christmas tree and then I'm bringing the kids back with me while you and Elle go shopping."

"We're going shopping?" I asked as I looked at Ellery.

"Do you have a problem with that?"

"The big game is on today, Elle. You knew that. That's why I wanted to go early and look for a tree and then get back."

"Oh. So what you're saying is that the game is more important than Christmas shopping with your wife for your children and family."

"Ellery Rose Black. That's not fair," I said as I ate my pancakes.

"Are you two going to fight?" Collin asked.

"Of course not, baby. Daddy's going with Mommy," she replied.

I sighed because I knew I didn't have a choice. I'd just make sure the place we went to for lunch had big-screen TVs everywhere.

"Julia, Collin, go upstairs and get yourselves dressed so we can go look for a Christmas tree."

They both got up and ran upstairs. As soon as Mason finished his pancakes, he went up to help them.

"What are we shopping for?" I asked Ellery as I helped her clean up the dishes.

"Presents for the kids and your family."

"We can't do that tomorrow?" I asked nicely.

"No. We're helping out at the soup kitchen. Remember?"

"That's tomorrow?" I asked.

"Yes. It's tomorrow and we'll be there all day."

Mason and the kids walked back into the kitchen. They were all bundled up and ready to go. "Okay, Black family, are you ready to search for the best Christmas tree ever?!"

"Yeah!" both kids exclaimed.

Ellery and I put on our coats and scarves before we headed down to the Range Rover.

"Connor, I'm sorry about the game. We can go shopping another time. I know you want to watch it." She smiled as she kissed my lips.

"It's okay, baby. We're going shopping."

"In that case, I'll make it up to you later tonight."

"Oh, I know you will." I winked as we climbed into the Range Rover and drove to the Christmas tree lot.

Ellery and I walked hand in hand as Mason walked in front of us with the kids. Growing up, my family never did this. My dad would call the tree lot and have them pick out the best tree they had and then have it delivered. My mom would call her decorators and they would come over and decorate it. I used to do that before Ellery. But then when she came into my life, all of that changed. We did things together and on our own, with no help from anyone. We wanted our children to have the best memories of us and their childhood by knowing that we did everything together as a family.

"Daddy, Daddy!" Julia exclaimed as she ran to a tree. "I love this one!" She smiled.

Mason and Collin walked over to another tree while Ellery and I looked over the one Julia liked. I walked around and examined it. It was pretty and nice and full.

"What do you think, Elle? Do you like it?"

"I think it's perfect." She smiled as she looped her arm around mine and laid her head on my shoulder.

I called for Mason to bring Collin over.

"Hey, buddy," I said as I picked him up. "Do you like this tree?"

"You better say yes or else," Julia said as she held up her fist to him.

"Julia Rose!" Ellery yelled as she looked at Mason.

"Princesses do not hold up their fists to people, Julia," Mason said. "Sorry."

"I like it, Daddy." Collin smiled as he grabbed my face.

"Excellent. Then this is the tree we shall buy."

I walked over to Ralph, the owner of the tree lot. "Happy holidays, Connor. Did you find a tree you like?"

7

"Happy holidays, Ralph. Yes, we did. We'll take this one," I said as I pointed to the tree.

"Best one on the lot!" He smiled.

"I picked it out," Julia said.

"Is that so? Well, you have a great eye for Christmas trees, Julia." She laughed and then proceeded to chase Collin around the lot, making Mason chase after them.

"Delivered, correct?"

"Yes, Ralph. How's tonight?"

"Tonight will be fine. Will someone be home?"

"If Ellery and I aren't, then Mason will be there."

"Okay, Connor. I'll just need cash or credit."

I reached in my wallet and pulled out my credit card. Ellery walked up behind me and wrapped her arms around my waist.

"I love this time of year. It reminds me of when you proposed to me on the beach in California."

"Best thing I've ever done in my life." I smiled as I turned around and kissed her.

We kissed the kids goodbye and Mason took them back to the penthouse while Ellery and I set off on our shopping adventure.

CHAPTER THREE

Ellery

"Where to first?" Connor asked while we were stuck in traffic. "Tiffany's." I smiled.

"And what are we buying at Tiffany's?" He smirked.

"Christmas gifts for your mom and sister. Tiffany has these amazing new bracelets and I know they'll love them. Oh, and there's a necklace that I want to get Peyton."

"Shouldn't Henry be buying her a necklace from Tiffany's?" he asked.

I glared at him.

"What?" he asked with a smile.

"For your information, Mr. Black, it's a 'best friends' necklace. So that means that a best friend buys it, not a husband."

He laughed. "Sorry, baby. I didn't know."

He parked the Range Rover and we walked down the street to Tiffany's. Before walking inside, we admired the beautiful pieces in the window.

"I want you to let me know if you see anything you like." Connor smiled.

"Are you saying you don't know what to buy me for Christmas?" I smiled back as I lightly tugged on his scarf.

"Of course not, baby."

We walked inside and were immediately greeted. I found it odd that Connor told the sales girl exactly what I was looking for and then disappeared. The two bracelets I looked at for Connor's mom and sister were perfect. I knew they were going to love them. The sales girl asked me if I was interested in anything else and I told her

9

about the necklace for Peyton. She walked me over to the other side of the store where the necklaces were displayed and that was when I saw Connor standing in the corner, staring at his phone in excitement. Oh my God; he was watching the game on his phone. That was why he asked me in the car what I was looking for so he could go to the opposite end of the store. Damn, he was good. I made my purchase and walked over to him. He saw me coming and quickly put his phone in his pocket and smiled.

"There you are. I've been looking everywhere for you. Why are you standing over here?"

"I had to take a business call. No big deal. Everything's fine."

"Good. So do I have your full attention now?" I smiled.

"Of course you do, baby. Did you see anything you wanted?"

"No," I said as we walked out of the store.

I pulled my phone from my purse and took my chances. "Oh my God, the Giants are losing by that much!"

"They are not! I just watched the last play and we were up by twenty," he said as he pulled out his phone.

"Oh, really?" I said as I stood and stared at him.

"I mean, I overheard people in Tiffany's talking about it."

"Really, Connor? Are you lying to me?"

He stood there and stared at me. I could see the wheels turning in his head while he debated very carefully what to say.

"Fine. I was watching the game while you were looking at jewelry and you know what, Elle? I'm not even going to apologize for it. What's the big deal anyway? So what if I watched a bit of it? Did I commit a crime? No, I don't think so."

I put my hand over his mouth and laughed. "Stop, Connor. I don't care. I just expect you to keep me updated on the score."

"Really?" he asked with relief.

"Come on; let's go to Neiman Marcus and then we can go to dinner and you can watch the rest of the game."

As we walked through the store, on our way to the girls' section to buy a holiday dress for Julia, I heard Connor call me from behind.

"Um, Elle? Come here."

I stopped and turned around and saw him standing in the middle of the lingerie section, looking at some Christmas nighties, bras, and panties. He had a big smile on his face.

"What are you doing?" I asked.

"I'm buying you one of these. Pick out which one you like."

"Connor, we're here to get Julia a dress." I smiled.

He took a Santa hat from the shelf and put it on my head. "Damn, that's getting me hard. You go to the girls' department and I'm going to pick something myself. Now go on," he said as he took the hat off of me.

"Seriously?"

"Yes, seriously. Now go. I'll meet you over there. Then, later tonight, you're going to model what I bought for you and I'm going to do very bad things to you while you're wearing it."

He had me wet already and I needed to get away from him or I was going to take him in the dressing room and make him fuck me. I didn't dare say that, though, because he wouldn't think twice about it.

"Okay. I'll be there in the girls' section. Don't take too long." I smiled.

As I was purchasing the dress for Julia, Connor walked up and stood next to me with a large bag in his hand.

"What did you buy?" I laughed. "That's a pretty big bag for a little piece of lingerie."

"Sweetheart, you know I don't do things in a small way. Tomorrow starts the twelve days of Christmas, so I bought twelve different pieces and we're going to start counting down the days; one outfit and one night at a time."

I heard the sales girl gasp and I watched her bite down on her bottom lip as she looked at Connor. "Now look what you did. You got this poor sales girl all wound up."

"Ellery," he said.

"I'm sorry. Here's your dress. Happy holidays."

I grabbed Connor's hand and led him out of the girls' department.

"You embarrassed that poor girl back there," he said.

"She embarrassed herself by looking at you like that, and you shouldn't have said such things in front of her."

He chuckled as he kissed the side of my head. "You love it and you know it."

CHAPTER FOUR

Connor

When we arrived back at the penthouse from a day full of shopping, I walked into the living room and saw the tree had been delivered. I turned on the fireplace and took a seat in my chair.

"Hi, Daddy," Julia said as she sat on my lap.

"Hi, princess. Did you have fun today with Uncle Mason?"

"Yes. Did you and Mommy have fun shopping?"

"Of course we did."

"Did you buy me anything? Like maybe that iPad I want with the Hello Kitty case?" She smiled as she placed her hand on my cheek.

"Princess, I thought you asked Santa Claus for that?"

"Come on, Daddy. We both know there's no Santa Claus."

"Julia! Of course there is."

"Daddy, please. I'm a big girl now. There's no need to pretend anymore."

"If you don't believe in Santa Claus, then I'm afraid you won't get any presents."

I couldn't believe my little princess and I were having this conversation.

"Yes, I will. You'll always buy me presents. Don't worry; I won't tell Collin. He can find out on his own."

"Julia, you better not tell your mother that you don't believe in Santa. She'll be crushed. Let's keep this our little secret." I winked.

"Okay, Daddy."

Ellery walked in the room and smiled at Julia. "I bought you a beautiful new dress for Christmas. Why don't you go upstairs and try it on for us."

"Okay, Mommy." She smiled as she jumped off my lap and ran up the stairs.

Ellery had a glass of wine in her hand and sat down on my lap. She brought the glass up to my lips and I took a sip.

"Are we going to decorate the tree tonight?" she asked.

"Sure. We can do it tonight."

"Then let's do it now. I'll call down and have the guys bring up all the boxes from storage." She smiled.

"Where's Collin?"

"He's up in his room, looking at that new Christmas book we bought him."

Ellery called downstairs. I got up from my seat and went to check on Collin.

"Hey, buddy. Are you ready to decorate the Christmas tree?"

"Yeah!" he said in excitement.

I picked him up, and before I carried him downstairs, I looked at him seriously.

"You believe in Santa Claus. Right?"

"Yeah. He brings me toys."

"Good boy," I said as I kissed his head.

"Is everyone ready?" I asked before plugging in the lights on the tree.

"Yes!" they all exclaimed.

I plugged the cord into the wall and the tree lit up like magic. The kids jumped up and down and I walked over to Ellery and stared at it with her.

"It's beautiful." She smiled as she kissed me.

"It certainly is."

"That's because I picked it out," Julia said.

"So did I," Collin commented.

"I saw it first and told Daddy that was the one I wanted. He just asked your opinion."

"Daddy, Mommy, tell Julia that I picked it out too."

I looked at Ellery and sighed. "It's time for bed, children. Get upstairs and change into your pajamas. It's been a long day and everyone's tired."

"You better not be too tired, Mr. Black. I still have something to try on." Ellery winked.

"Baby, I'm never too tired for you."

I couldn't wait anymore. I had been fantasizing about Ellery in one of the outfits I bought her all day long. "Kids, let's go. NOW!"

"Gee, Daddy. We're going. You don't have to yell," Julia said as she narrowed her eyes at me and walked away in a huff.

"I didn't yell, princess."

Ellery and I tucked the kids into bed and went to our bedroom and locked the door. We started our twelve days of Christmas a day early.

Since it was Sunday, I decided to get up early and make breakfast for the family. As I started the coffee, Julia walked in the kitchen.

"Good morning, princess."

"Morning, Daddy. Whatcha doing?"

"Making French toast."

"Can I help?"

"You sure can, princess. Go get the bread from the pantry."

As I made the egg mixture and started to heat the pan, Julia brought the bread over.

"What's going on in here?" Ellery smiled as she walked in the kitchen with Collin.

"Me and Daddy are making French toast, so go sit down and we'll bring you some."

Ellery smiled as she walked over, grabbed a cup of coffee, and kissed me on the cheek. Julia and I made the French toast together and we had a great Sunday breakfast, just the four of us. After breakfast, we got the children ready and we headed to the soup kitchen to help out for the day.

CHAPTER FIVE

After Connor left for the office, I called Peyton.

"Good morning, Elle."

"Good morning. I need your help."

"With?"

"I don't know what to get Connor for Christmas. The man has everything."

"Just slap a bow on your naked body. That'll be good enough for him." She laughed.

"Ugh. Peyton, I'm serious."

"I don't know, Elle. Is there anything he wants?"

"No. That's the problem."

"Whisk him away somewhere for a few days. Just the two of you."

"That's a great idea!"

Connor had been talking for the past year about wanting to take a trip to Colorado in the winter to do some skiing and snowboarding. He had never been snowboarding, but he always wanted to try it. I got online, made some phones calls, and booked our trip for December twenty-sixth. I took care of everything. I even booked our flight. Not on the company plane, of course, because then he'd know. I booked us two first-class tickets to Colorado. I was so excited because this was going to be such a surprise to him. As I was doing my happy dance around the living room, Mason walked in.

"What are we celebrating?" He smiled as he danced with me.

"I finally figured out what to get Connor for Christmas!"

"Oh, yay! Do tell."

"I booked us a trip to Aspen for skiing and snowboarding. I already booked the snowboarding lessons."

"How romantic. The two of you in some secluded little cabin, sitting by the fire, wrapped in a blanket and keeping each other warm while the tea kettle is heating up water for some hot tea."

I looked at him with a twisted face. "I booked us a room at the St. Regis Resort. Oh shit; should I have done a little cabin thingy?"

"Nah. The St. Regis will be perfect for the both of you. I was just telling you my dream Colorado vacation."

I laughed as I poked his arm. "Let's go shopping. I need to buy clothes and jackets and scarves and hats. I'll wrap them up separately and give them to Connor for Christmas and then the last gift will be our reservation for the trip. I'll have him open his gloves first." I smiled.

"Let's go to Paragon Sports over in Union Square. They have the most amazing selections there," Mason said with excitement.

"Awesome. Let's go."

Denny was driving Connor around town today from one meeting to another, so Mason and I took a cab. When we walked into Paragon Sports, we headed straight to the ski department. As we were looking for ski wear, my phone starting to ring. Shit. It was Connor calling.

"Hi, babe," I answered.

"Hey, baby. What are you doing?"

"Just doing some Christmas shopping with Mason."

"So you're not home?" he asked.

"No. I won't be home until later. Why?"

"No reason. I'm on my way home and was going to pick up dinner."

"Mason and I will probably grab something while we're out. Why don't you order a pizza for you and the kids?"

"Will do, sweetheart. I'll see you later. Have fun shopping. I love you."

"I love you too. Bye, babe."

I hit the end button and looked at Mason. "Okay. Where were we?"

We walked arm in arm through the store and picked up ski jackets, ski pants, boots, beanies, helmets, goggles, gloves, thermal polo necks, sunglasses, ski socks, and a couple of wool sweaters for Connor. I was in ski heaven and so excited.

"Elle, come here! You must try on this fuchsia ski jacket. It will look fab on you."

I walked over and took it from the hanger and tried it on. Mason put his hands over his mouth.

"You are so buying that. It looks amazing on you, girl!"

"It is adorable, isn't it?" I smiled as I turned and looked at myself in the mirror.

The salesman took the jacket along with everything else I was purchasing up to the register. I smiled as I handed him my credit card.

"Won't Connor see the statement?" Mason asked.

"It won't come until after Christmas."

The salesman handed me my card and asked when I wanted everything delivered.

"Tomorrow during the day will be good."

"You're all set, Mrs. Black. You'll be our first delivery tomorrow morning at nine a.m."

"Thank you. Please make sure it's not before nine because my husband will still be home."

We walked out of the store and headed to the Japanese restaurant down the street for dinner. When I arrived home, I found Connor sitting in his office.

"I'm home." I smiled.

"How was shopping?" he asked as he held out his arms.

I walked over to him and sat down on his lap. "It was fun."

"Where are all your bags?"

"Since we took a cab, I'm having everything delivered."

"Good idea. So what did you buy?"

"Just some things for the kids, Denny and Dana, Valerie, Camden, your dad."

"Well, it sounds like you got a lot done." He smiled as he brushed his lips against mine.

"Are the kids sleeping?" I asked.

"Yep. They were exhausted."

"If you don't mind, I'm going to take a bath and then put on one of the outfits you bought me. We are celebrating the twelve days of Christmas, don't forget."

"Believe me, it's all I thought about all day. I have your outfit hanging on the door. I'll be waiting for you in bed when you get out of the bathtub."

I kissed my sexy and unforgettable husband before going upstairs and preparing for a most fulfilling night of pleasure.

CHAPTER SIX

Connor

I sat in my office, deliriously happy that I finished up Ellery for Christmas. She was going to love what I bought her. I could hardly wait to see the expression on her face. As I was working on some contracts, my phone rang. It was my mom.

"Hello, Mom."

"Hello, Connor. I'm calling about Christmas. You, Ellery, and the kids will be coming on Christmas day, correct?"

"Yes, Mom. Just like we do every year."

"Just making sure. I want all of my family here."

"You're coming to the Black Enterprises Christmas party, aren't you? Valerie just told me today you hadn't mentioned it."

"Yes. Your father and I will be there, honey. When is it again?"

"This Saturday evening at six o'clock at the Waldorf."

"Okay. See you then. Give Ellery and my precious grandbabies big kisses from me and your dad."

"I will, Mom." I hung up and smiled, and then I dialed Ellery.

"Hi, lover. What's up?" she answered.

"Hi, baby. I was hoping to take Collin and Julia ice skating tonight."

"By yourself?"

"No. You can come if you want." I laughed.

"Let me check my schedule. Hold on. Okay; I can go."

"You're too cute."

"Seriously, I think the kids would love it. I'll make sure they're ready when you get home and we can go and then grab something to eat after."

20

"Sounds good. I love you, Elle."

"I love you too. Bye."

As much as I loved the warm weather and going to the beach house in the summer, I loved this time of year even more. The lights, the trees, the holiday decorations, and just the overall celebrating made me incredibly happy. I finished up with the contracts I was looking over, grabbed my coat, and met Denny outside to go home.

"How was your day, Connor?"

"It was good, Denny. You know I love this time of year," I said with a smile on my face.

"Yeah, for only about the past eight years." He laughed.

"Regardless, I love it. I'm taking Ellery and the kids ice skating tonight. Why don't you come with us?"

"No thanks. The last time I went ice skating, I couldn't move for a week."

"That's because you're an old man." I chuckled.

"You better watch it. You're getting up there in age too. Did you get everything set for Ellery for Christmas?"

"Yes, and I can hardly wait."

We arrived home and Denny came up with me to have a cup of coffee and see Ellery and the kids before he went home for the night.

"Uncle Denny," Julia said as she hugged him. "Guess what? We're going ice skating."

"I know. Your daddy told me. You be careful and have lots of fun."

Collin came running into the kitchen and sat on Denny's lap. "Hello, Connor Jr."

Collin giggled.

"Have you decided what you want to be when you grow up?" he asked.

"My daddy," Collin answered.

"Well, let's hope not. At least not the 'before-Ellery Connor.'"

"Denny!" I said.

"What? I don't want to go through that again and, believe me, I'll be around as he grows up."

Ellery walked into the kitchen, laughing. "It's always a pleasure to see you, Denny," she said as she kissed his cheek.

We sat on the bench in Rockefeller Center and I helped Julia lace up her skates. Ellery helped Collin and, once we were ready, we took their hands and led them out onto the ice. Julia skated off and I took Collin's other hand. Julia was a little pro, but Collin was still wobbly. It was cold out and it was snowing lightly. It was the perfect night.

"Do you remember years ago when we came here with Peyton and Henry and I told you that we'd bring our children here one day?"

Ellery looked over at me and smiled. "Yes. I do remember."

"Tonight reminds me of that night, and look; we brought our children."

She leaned over and gave me a soft kiss. We both laughed as Collin stared up at us, making a face.

"Come on, Mommy," Julia said as she skated by us and grabbed Ellery's hand.

As they skated in front of us, I couldn't help but smile as I stared at my two beautiful and breathtaking girls.

"I'm hungry," Julia said as she and Ellery skated over to the rail where I was holding Collin.

"Me too," Collin said.

"Then let's get these skates off and go get something to eat." I smiled.

"I want to eat at the Shake Shack, Daddy," Julia announced.

Ellery laughed because she knew I wasn't fond of that place.

"And what are you going to get there that you can't get somewhere else, princess?" I asked as I unlaced her skates.

"A hot dog."

"You can get a hot dog anywhere."

"Not like the ones there, Daddy. I want the hot dog with the cheese sauce." She smiled.

Instantly, my stomach churned. Ellery was trying to hold back the laughter as she took off Collin's skates.

"I want a hot dog too," Collin pouted.

"Okay, then I guess we're going to the Shake Shack."

"Yay!" both kids exclaimed with excitement.

Ellery put her arm around me and gave me a kiss on my cheek. "You're such a good daddy." She laughed.

We sat in a booth at the Shake Shack and I watched as Julia took a bite of her hot dog and cheese sauce started dripping down her chin. I shook my head as I handed her a napkin.

"Here, Daddy; taste it," she said as she held the hot dog up to me.

"No, no, Julia. I don't want to taste it."

"Yes, you do." She smiled as she brought it closer to my mouth.

"Do it, Dad." Collin laughed.

As I stared at her and the smile on her face, I realized that she reminded me so much of Ellery. I looked across the table. She was smiling at me because she was also remembering the time when she first shoved a hot dog in my face.

"Fine," I said as I took a bite.

"Isn't it the best, Daddy?!" Julia smiled.

"It sure is," I said as I chewed up the hot dog with the cheese sauce I so desperately wanted to spit out.

CHAPTER SEVEN

Ellery

I opened my eyes and saw Connor standing in the closet, pulling out one of his business suits. He had a towel wrapped around his waist and his hair was wet. As I looked over at the clock and saw it was fifteen minutes after eight, I freaked out.

"Oh my God, Connor. Why is it after eight and why are you not dressed and ready for the office?" I flew out of bed and into the bathroom. "How did I sleep so late?"

"Ellery, why are you freaking out? The kids don't have school today. Remember? And I have a meeting downtown at ten o'clock. I thought it was nice we got to sleep in."

I frantically brushed my teeth, listening to what he was saying. Sure, it all would have been good on any other day, but not today. His Christmas gifts were being delivered at nine o'clock!

As I walked out of the bathroom and towards the closet, Connor grabbed my arm and pulled me into him.

"In fact, we have a little bit of time for me to pleasure you." He smiled as his lips grazed my neck.

I pulled away. "No."

"No? What do you mean no? What's wrong with you?"

SHIT. I had to think. "I'm sorry, Connor. It's just I have really bad cramps and I need to get downstairs and take something."

"You were fine last night."

"That was last night. Now it's morning. A different day and I have cramps," I said as I pulled up my jeans and threw on a sweater.

I raced out of the room and down the stairs to the kitchen, where my phone was sitting on the counter. I dialed Denny.

"Good morning, Ellery."

"Denny, I need you over here now, and I need you to get Connor out of the penthouse."

"What's wrong?"

"All his Christmas presents are being delivered at nine o'clock. He was supposed to be gone already. I didn't know he had a meeting at ten. Please make up something and get him out of here."

"Calm down, Ellery. I'm on my way."

As soon as I set down my phone, Connor walked in the kitchen.

"Were you just talking to someone?" He poured himself a cup of coffee.

"Umm. I just tried to call Peyton but she didn't answer, so I left her a voice message. Are the kids still sleeping?"

"No. They're on their way down. Did you take something for your cramps?"

"I'm doing that right now," I replied as I walked to the cabinet and took out the bottle of Motrin.

"We're hungry, Mommy," Julia said as she and Collin walked into the kitchen and sat at the table next to Connor.

"Breakfast is coming right up and good morning to both of you."

Collin got up from his chair and ran over and gave me a hug. "Morning, Mommy."

"Sorry, Mom. Good morning."

I looked at the clock on the stove as I was getting the boxes of cereal out of the pantry and panicking. It was now eight forty-five. *Where was Denny?*

"Good morning, Black family," Denny said.

Thank God.

"Denny, you're early."

"Come on, Connor; let's go."

"We don't have to leave for another forty-five minutes. I'm just about to have breakfast."

"That's the reason I'm here early. I thought maybe you and I could have breakfast together this morning. There's that great diner downtown that serves those amazing Belgian waffles."

25

I looked over at Connor as he sipped his coffee. "Great idea. You should go. It's been a while since the two of you went out."

"We can go another time, Denny. Sit down and have breakfast with us."

I slammed the box of cereal down on the counter. "All you're getting is cereal, Connor! I'm not making anything else!"

He looked at me, and as he narrowed his eyes, he took in a breath. "Right. Come on, Denny. Let's go to that diner."

I let out a sigh of relief. Connor got up from his seat, put on his suit coat, and walked over and kissed my head. "Have a good day, baby, and try not to break anything while I'm gone."

The minute he stepped onto the elevator and the doors shut, the delivery man was at the front door and so was Mason.

"Oh thank God," I said as I pulled Mason into the penthouse. "Go in the kitchen and distract the kids. You know Little Miss Tells Daddy Everything will tell him if she sees these."

"I'm on it." He smiled.

I showed the delivery man to the small storage room that was off the foyer and towards the back of the penthouse. It was a room Connor and I used at Christmas time to hide the kids' presents. We kept it locked and I was the only one who had the key. I instructed him to put all of the presents in there and then I gave him a large tip.

"Thank you, Mrs. Black. Happy holidays to you and your family."

"Happy holidays to you too. Thank you."

I shut the door and sighed with relief. It was only nine fifteen and I was already exhausted.

"Connor is going to be thrilled when he finds out you booked a trip for the two of you to Colorado," Peyton said as she pulled a dress from the rack.

"I hope so."

"Are you spending New Year's Eve there?"

"Yes. We'll be coming home on New Year's Day. How's this one?" I asked as I pulled out a red Valentino cocktail dress.

"Amazing! You need to try that on."

"I wish you and Henry could come to the holiday party at Black Enterprises," I pouted.

"Me too. Of all nights for Henry's parents to be flying in. But we'll be at your house on Christmas Eve."

Every Christmas Eve, Connor and I had a small get-together at the penthouse with our closest friends. I stepped into the fitting room and tried on the red dress. When I walked out to show Peyton, she smiled.

"Perfect. You look super sexy in it and Connor will be walking around with a hard-on all night."

"I do love it. You don't think it's cut too low, do you?"

"Hell no. You've got the boobs, Elle. Show those babies off, and if Connor says something about it, then just tell him he won't be having them later."

I laughed. "Fine. Now I need to find the perfect shoes."

We shopped for a couple more hours and then Peyton had to get home to Hailey. When I stepped off the elevator and walked into the living room, Mason, Julia, and Collin were all playing Twister.

"Thank God you're home," Mason said, looking like he was in agony. He untwisted himself and stepped off the mat.

"Hey, we aren't finished yet," Julia said.

"Princess, you're killing your Uncle Mason. I can only bend and twist so far."

She giggled.

"Come upstairs with me. I have to show you the dress I bought for the office party. Julia, Collin, why don't the two of you go play some video games?"

Julia took hold of Collin's hand and led him upstairs. "Okay, Mommy."

Mason followed me into the bedroom as I lifted the plastic bag from the dress. He whistled.

"That dress is fabulous. Oh, and it's a Valentino. Shoes?"

"Of course I bought shoes." I smiled as I took the Manolo red pumps from the box.

"Perfect, Elle. Just perfect! Connor is going to love it. Except he may say something about the dress being so low cut."

"He won't say anything. He knows better. I think."

Mason laughed, kissed me on the cheek, and went to check on the kids. I hung my dress in the closet and sighed, for I knew Connor was going to have a problem with it.

CHAPTER EIGHT

Connor

"You never told me if you found a dress for the holiday party," I said as I ran on the treadmill next to her.

"Why are you thinking about that?"

"Why not? Usually, you show me if you bought something and you haven't shown me anything. The party is tomorrow night."

"I bought a dress." She smiled as she looked over at me.

"Why haven't you shown me yet?"

"Because it's a surprise. I want to wow you with it on."

Something wasn't sitting right with her answer. "Am I going to have a problem with the dress?"

"Why would you ask that?"

"Because, usually, you always show me right when you buy it."

"Damn it, Connor. It's a surprise. Can't I surprise my husband?"

I sighed. I already knew that she was hiding something and I'd better brace myself when I saw it on her. Ellery got off the treadmill and walked over to the weight machine. I followed behind, wiping my face with a towel. I climbed on the machine next to her.

"Baby, I know you're hiding something."

"Drop it, Black. I'm not hiding anything. I want to surprise you, but if you can't handle it, then I guess I won't go."

Oh God, when she talked like that, she was serious. I sighed as I told her the subject was dropped and got up and went into the locker room. I pulled my phone from my bag and called Peyton.

"Hey, Connor. What's up?"

"You were with Ellery when she purchased her dress for the holiday party. Right?"

"Yes." She giggled.

"She won't show me. Do I need to be worried?"

"It's so beautiful, Connor. She probably just wants to surprise you. I'm gathering by your phone call that the two of you are arguing about it."

"I wouldn't call it arguing, but she still won't talk about it."

"Connor, prepare yourself to be in awe and walk around all night with a hard-on. It's going to take a lot of restraint for you to keep your hands to yourself."

"Great. Thanks, Peyton."

She giggled as she hung up.

I walked back out to main area of the gym and over the weight machine where Ellery was. I leaned over and kissed her.

"Are you mad at me?"

"Nope." She smiled.

"Then show me."

She stopped and looked at me. "Huh?"

"Show me you're not mad at me."

"Where?" She glared at me.

"Steam room."

"It's too hot in there."

"Hot tub."

"If it was ours, fine, but it's a public hot tub."

"What's your point? Imagine the jets, Ellery." I smiled.

The corners of her mouth curved up. "Fine. Hot tub it is."

She got up and headed towards the room where the hot tub was. I informed the staff of the gym that we wanted to be alone and no one was allowed in there.

After leaving the gym, Ellery and I spent the rest of the day finishing up the Christmas shopping. We walked into the Apple Store to buy Julia the iPad she so desperately wanted.

"We have a problem," Ellery said.

"What?" I asked as I was looking at the iPads.

"There is no Hello Kitty case."

"No problem, baby. We'll find one."

As I was waiting for the salesman to get the iPad and check us out, I pulled up Hello Kitty cases on my phone and nobody seemed to have them in stock. I was confused because this was Hello Kitty. The salesman handed me the bag and I asked him about the case.

"We had some and sold out the day they came in. That's a pretty hot case this year. See what's happening is parents are buying their kids iPads at a younger age and the younger girls are all into Hello Kitty. Good luck in trying to find one."

Ellery looked at me with "the look."

"Okay. It's not my fault that they don't have it," I said as we walked out of the store.

"Yes it is. I told you a month ago that I would go and buy it for her while I was out and your exact words were: 'Oh no, Elle. I'll pick it up for our princess. You do enough. Don't worry about it. I'll take care of it.' Well, here were are now because you never did it."

"Always my fault, Elle. Always my fault."

"Don't deny it. It *is* your fault."

"Don't worry, baby. I'll find our daughter a Hello Kitty iPad case."

She was pissed off. It wasn't like I forgot. I just thought it wouldn't be a problem. Ellery checked her phone and it said that FAO Schwarz had some in stock, so we headed there. The place was a madhouse. One week before Christmas and I swear the entire city of New York was in the store. We made our way to the area that sold the iPad covers and asked the sales girl if they had any.

"Oh, I'm sorry. That lady that just left here bought the last one."

Ellery ran and caught up with her. "Excuse me, ma'am."

"Yes," the lady said as she turned around and stood in front of us.

"We want that iPad case." Ellery smiled.

The woman clutched her bag tightly to her chest. "You're crazy. Do you know how hard these are to find? No way. My kid has been wanting this all year."

"My kid wants it too," Ellery snapped.

"Excuse me," I interrupted. "What my wife is trying to say is that we would like to buy that from you. I'll pay you double the cost."

She looked at me, and then at Ellery. "I'm sorry, but no. I won't disappoint my son at Christmas."

Son? Did she just say son?

"Son? What does your son want with a Hello Kitty case? And besides, it's pink," Ellery said.

She was going to ruin this chance, so I needed to take control. I put my arm around the woman and walked her slowly away from Ellery.

"Listen, my daughter is seven years old and she's expecting this Hello Kitty iPad case to go with her new iPad. How about we do this? I'm going to offer you one hundred dollars for your case."

She looked me up and down. "If you want it that badly, then it's going to cost you three hundred dollars. It's a hot commodity, you know."

I pulled out my wallet. "Fine. Here you go. Three hundred dollars."

"Thank you." She smiled as she handed me the bag. "Merry Christmas."

Ellery walked over to me and shook her head. "How much?"

"Three hundred."

"Have you learned your lesson?" she asked with a smirk.

I sighed and walked away.

We arrived home and Mason left. I walked into the living room and found Julia sitting in front of the tree, staring at it.

"What are you doing, princess?" I asked as I sat down next to her.

"Just thinking."

"About what?"

"This girl I met today at the coffee shop that Uncle Mason took me and Collin to."

"What about her?"

"She was coloring at one of the tables and I walked over and sat across from her and told her that she colored pretty. She told me that her mom was the lady behind the counter and that she makes the coffee. I asked her what she was getting for Christmas and she said nothing because they couldn't afford it. She said her mom promised her that as soon as she got her overtime check in January, she'd buy her something real nice."

I put my arm around her. "Princess, that's sad."

"Daddy, I want to do something for her and her mom for Christmas. It's not fair."

"I know it's not, princess, and that's very nice of you to want to help them. I'll tell you what – let me think about it for a day and we'll discuss it. Okay?"

"Okay, Daddy." She smiled as she hugged me. "Oh, by the way, I don't think I want that Hello Kitty case anymore. I may want something different."

I squeezed my little girl a little too tight as I gritted my teeth.

"Ouch, Daddy. You squeezed me too tight."

"Sorry, princess."

After finishing up some work in my office, I went upstairs, checked to make sure the kids were sleeping, and then headed to the bedroom, where Ellery was taking a bubble bath in the master bathroom.

"So your daughter told me that she doesn't think she wants the Hello Kitty iPad case anymore," I said as I unbuttoned my shirt.

"What? Why?"

"She said she may want something different."

"Well, that's just too bad. It's a week before Christmas and she just can't change her mind like that, especially since her very spoiling father gave some woman three hundred dollars for one."

"I agree, Ellery. I completely agree. Now, I want you to wear this tonight." I smiled as I held up her lingerie and then hung it on the knob of the bathroom door.

CHAPTER NINE

Ellery

I rolled over and smiled as I watched Connor sleeping peacefully. I quietly got out of bed, slipped on my robe, and went downstairs to the kitchen. It was seven a.m. and the kids were still asleep. If I hurried up, I could get at least one cup of coffee down before they woke up. I started a pot of coffee and, as it was brewing, Connor walked in, holding Collin. *There goes my one cup of coffee,* I thought.

"Good morning, my sweet men." I smiled as I kissed them both.

"Morning, baby."

"Hi, Mommy."

"Where's Julia?" I asked.

"She's still sleeping," Connor replied.

He put Collin down and told him to go play in the living room and we'd call him when breakfast was ready.

"Go sit down. I'll make breakfast today," he said.

"Are you sure? I can make it."

The coffee was finished brewing and Connor poured some into a cup, handed it to me, and then kissed my forehead.

"Go sit down and relax. Are you ready for the party tonight?"

"I think so. Roger is coming over at three o'clock for hair and makeup. I have my dress, my shoes, and my jewelry. So yeah, I'm ready." I smiled.

"About that dress. Do you think I could just see it? Please, Ellery. Please."

He was driving me insane about the dress. He was so damn worried about me looking too sexy in it and other men staring at me; men that worked for him. Did he really think his employees are that stupid?

"Fine, Connor. I'll go try it on for you right now," I said as I got up from my chair.

"Really?"

"Yes, really."

I walked upstairs and pulled the dress from the back of the closet. I slipped into it and put on my shoes. When I walked into the kitchen, Julia was sitting at the table and she looked at me.

"Mommy, you look beautiful."

Connor turned around and his mouth dropped. "Oh, hell no, Ellery."

"No what, Daddy? Doesn't Mommy look beautiful?"

"Yes, she does, princess. Too beautiful. Now go take that off. I'll call Mason to come watch the kids and I'll take you shopping for a new dress. We can take that one back."

You would think by now that my husband would know better, but obviously he hadn't learned yet after all these years.

"No need to take me. You stay with the kids and I'll go," I said as I turned around and went upstairs.

A few moments later, Connor walked into the bedroom. "Are you mad at me, Ellery? It's just that dress is too low cut and, with your amazing tits and your perfect body, people are going to be staring at you and it'll make me very uncomfortable."

Oh he had no idea how uncomfortable he was going to be feeling. "I understand, Connor," I said as I slipped on my jeans and a shirt.

"You do?" he asked in confusion.

"Yep. Now if you'll excuse me, I have to finish getting ready so I can get to the stores right when they open."

"I'll go with you. I really want to."

"No need. You stay with the children. I'll be back before you know it." I smiled as I kissed his lips.

He walked out of the room and I dialed Peyton.

"Morning, Elle."

"Morning. I tried on that dress for Connor. He blew a fit and said I wasn't wearing it. Can you meet me downtown in about an hour?"

"What are you doing downtown?"

"There are a couple vintage stores I want to check out."

"Oh, how fun! I know what you're up to and I love it. I'll meet you there in an hour!"

After we hung up, I fixed my hair and put on my makeup. When I walked into the kitchen, Collin, Connor, and Julia were all sitting at the table.

"I'm off, my little munchkins," I said as I kissed Julia and Collin goodbye. "I'll be back in a while," I said as I started to walk out.

"Excuse me, but where's my kiss?" Connor said.

"You don't get one." I smiled.

As I turned to walk out, I heard Julia giggle and say, "Uh oh, I think Daddy's in trouble."

Peyton and I were looking through the racks of dresses and, to my surprise, they really didn't have anything.

"I don't think you're going to find the perfect ugly dress here," Peyton said.

"I think you're right. Let's try somewhere else."

We left the store and walked down the street. We came across a Salvation Army store.

"Perfect!" Peyton smiled as she grabbed my hand and we went inside.

She started on one rack of dresses and I started on another. Then I found it. The perfect dress for Connor.

"Peyton, look!" I exclaimed as I held up the long brown and yellow floral dress with a large collar and buttons all the way up to the neck.

"God, that is one hideous dress and, on you, it will even look worse. Poor Connor; you'd think he'd know by now not to piss you off and to stop being so controlling."

"I guess he'll learn tonight. Won't he?" I smiled. Since I didn't eat, Peyton and I grabbed some brunch before heading home. "Thank you for meeting me," I said.

"You're welcome. I wouldn't have missed this for the world. Make sure to video Connor's reaction and send it to me."

"I will."

"Have fun tonight in that sexy red dress of yours."

"I fully intend to now." I smiled.

When I arrived back at the penthouse, Connor came walking out of his office when he heard the elevator doors open.

"You found something, I see," he said.

"I did and I promise you'll like it."

"Can I see it?" he asked.

"Seriously, Connor. This dress is really amazing and I swear to you that I'm not trying to hide it, but I really want you to see me in it after my hair and makeup are done. I'm really excited about this dress. I just wish I would have seen it before I purchased the other one."

He walked over to me and put his hands on my hips. "That makes me very happy that you found one you like and that you know I'll like better."

"You'll love this dress, babe." I smiled as I brushed my lips against his.

"Good; I can't wait to see it on you."

Oh, and I can't wait until he sees it on me either. I smiled to myself as I took the dress upstairs.

I was up in my bedroom when Connor brought Roger upstairs.

"Hi, Roger." I smiled as I walked over and kissed him.

"Are you ready to look fabulous for your holiday party?" he asked.

"I sure am."

Connor left the room and shut the door. "I need to see what you're wearing so I can coordinate hair and makeup."

I walked over to the closet and pulled out the dress I purchased from the Salvation Army.

"I'm wearing this tonight."

A look of horror swept across his face. "That's not even funny, Elle."

"This is the dress Connor thinks I'm wearing, but this is the actual dress I'm going to wear," I said as I pulled out the red Valentino.

Roger put his hands over his mouth. "It's amazing! I've got the perfect hairstyle for that dress." He took a moment and then cocked his head. "Wait, let me guess. Connor said you're not wearing that because it's too sexy."

"And the prize goes to the phenomenal hair and makeup artist, Roger!"

"Ugh, Elle. So has he seen the hideous dress yet? Because I can guarantee that he won't let you wear that one either."

"No. He hasn't seen it. I told him it was a total surprise and he's going to love it."

"I love the way you think. Come on; let's start your hair."

When we were in the bathroom and Roger was finishing up my hair, Mason walked in.

"Hello, my beautiful queen. Hello, Roger," he said as he kissed us both. "Sexy daddy said you were up here getting your hair and makeup done."

"Go into my closet and pull out the dress with the black bag over it," I said.

Roger started to chuckle.

"What the fuck is this?" Mason said as he lifted the bag.

"My new dress that I'm wearing tonight." I smiled.

"Sexy daddy had a problem with the Valentino, didn't he?"

"He did. So I went out this morning and found something more appropriate."

"Honey, I don't even think this dress would look appropriate on a homeless person."

"Exactly," Roger said.

"Well, I for one can't wait to hear the yelling once you put it on. I'll be downstairs with the prince and princess. Call me if you need me."

Roger laughed as he started my makeup.

A little while later, Connor walked in and grabbed his tuxedo from the closet. "You look so beautiful, Ellery." He smiled as Roger put the finishing touches on my eyes. "I can't wait to see you in your new dress."

Roger almost busted out into laughter until I smacked him on the leg.

"I'm going to go change in the other room. Call me when you have your dress on."

"Oh, I will, babe. Don't worry."

"You're finished. What do you think?" Roger asked.

"Amazing. This look is perfect for my red dress. Thank you, Roger."

"You're welcome, Elle. I'll be downstairs with Mason, waiting for the most anticipated reaction of the evening."

I sighed. "Wish me luck."

He walked out of the bedroom and I slipped into the ugly dress. As I looked in the mirror, I shook my head in disbelief and slipped my feet into a pair of old brown flats I had. I didn't even know why I kept them. They were just as ugly as the dress.

A few moments later, Connor lightly knocked on the door.

"Ellery, are you dressed?"

"I sure am. Come in." I smiled as I faced the mirror.

The door opened and Connor walked in. "What the fuck are you wearing?" he said with a raised voice.

"What? You don't like it?" I said in a sad tone.

"Ellery, what the hell are you doing or trying to pull? That is the ugliest dress I've ever seen and there's no way you would wear something like that."

"So what are you saying, Connor? Are you saying that I look hideous in this dress?"

"Yes! That's exactly what I'm saying. Now take that off and change into something else. You are not leaving the house in that."

I walked over to him and pressed my finger into his chest. "I am wearing this dress and if you don't like it, then you can go to your company party and explain to all your guests why your loving wife isn't by your side; especially your family."

I stormed out of the bedroom with a small smile on my face. As I walked into the living room, Mason and Roger bother started laughing.

"Mommy, that dress is ugly. Where's that pretty red one you had on this morning?"

"Oh my God, Elle." Mason laughed.

"I think you look pretty, Mommy," Collin said as he wrapped his arms around me.

"Thank you, Collin."

"Ellery, can you please come upstairs?" Connor said from behind.

"Sorry, Connor, but Denny will be here in a minute and we don't have time to have a discussion. So hurry up and finish getting ready so we can leave. I would hate for the owner of Black Enterprises to be late to his own holiday party."

I walked into the kitchen and Connor followed behind. He picked me up and threw me over his shoulder.

"Connor! Put me down."

"You forced my hand on this, Ellery."

He carried me up the stairs and, once we got to the bedroom, he kicked the door shut behind him and set me on the bed. He walked into the closet and pulled out the red dress.

"Put this on. You've made your point. I apologize."

I sat there as I arched my eyebrow. "I'm mad at you. I really am and, to be honest, I don't know when I'm not going to be mad at you anymore." I got up from the bed, grabbed the dress out of his hand, and went into the bathroom, shutting the door behind me. Once I changed, I went over to my jewelry box and put on the jewelry that went with my dress. I could feel Connor's eyes staring at me.

"We need to go," he said as he put on his coat.

When I walked downstairs, I kissed the kids goodbye and told them to be good for Mason.

"That's better, Mommy. You look like a princess," Julia said.

"Thank you, my darling. Be good for Uncle Mason and I'll see you tomorrow. Don't forget that we're spending the night at the hotel."

"I know. Have fun."

I stepped onto the elevator and let the doors shut while Connor was saying goodbye to the kids. Denny was waiting for us with the limo door open.

"Let me guess. You and Connor are arguing." He sighed.

"Yep, and it's all over my dress."

"So nothing new, then," he replied.

Connor climbed in next to me and shut the door. "Thank you for leaving without me. Is this how it's going to be all night?"

"How many years have we been together? How many times have you tried to stop me from wearing something and how many times have you failed? We've discussed this before. I'm mad at you, so please leave me alone and don't think you're getting sex for a long time, mister."

He sighed. "Okay, Ellery. If this is how you want it, then fine."

We arrived at the Waldorf and Connor made his rounds. I kept catching him staring at me from across the room. After we ate dinner, a slow song began to play and Connor's father asked me to dance. As we were dancing, Connor walked up.

"Excuse me, Dad. Do you mind if I dance with my incredibly beautiful wife?"

"Of course not, son."

Connor took my hand and placed his other around my waist. "You know how turned on I get when you pretend to be mad at me."

"Who says I'm pretending?"

"Oh, you are, Mrs. Black. Between your teasing and this dress, I've been hard all night, and I think we need to sneak up to our room for a bit and do something about it."

He leaned his lips closer to my ear and whispered, "I need to fuck you."

His warm breath on my neck sent chills throughout my body. "What are you waiting for?" I whispered.

He smiled as he took my hand and we took the elevator up to our suite, barely making it to the bed before he was inside me.

CHAPTER TEN

Connor

A s I lay there and watched Ellery sleep, I couldn't stop think-ing about how much I loved her and how excited she was going to be with her Christmas gift. Last night's party was excellent and everything turned out better than I had planned. Everyone had a great time and they were thrilled with the bonuses I gave out this year. Ellery opened her eyes as I stroked her beautiful blonde hair.

"Good morning." She smiled.

"Good morning." I leaned down and softly brushed my lips against hers.

"I'm starving."

"I already ordered room service. It'll be here in about thirty minutes."

"Thank you."

"You're welcome, my love. So, there's something I need to talk to you about."

Ellery climbed out of bed and went into the bathroom. "What about?"

"Something Julia told me the other day about a little girl she met at the coffee shop."

"What did she tell you?" Ellery asked as she put on her robe.

"Room service," we heard as there was a knock at the door.

"Hold that thought," I said as I pulled on my pajama bottoms and opened the door.

"Here you are, Mr. and Mrs. Black. Enjoy your breakfast."

"Thank you." I smiled as I tipped him.

I took a seat at the table across from Ellery and proceeded to tell her about the little girl at the coffee shop.

"That's really sad, Connor. What are you thinking of doing?"

"I don't know. I can't just walk up to her and hand her a check. You know how weird people can get about that sort of thing. I'll call the owner tomorrow when I get to the office in the morning."

"Since the kids are off from school now for Christmas vacation, I'll take Julia to the coffee shop tomorrow morning and she can show me the little girl's mom."

"Great idea, Elle. You find out her name and then call me."

My cell phone started to ring. It was Mason calling. "It's Mason," I said as I looked at Ellery. "Hello."

"Hi, Daddy."

I put the call on speaker. "Hello, princess."

"I was giving something a lot of thought and I needed to call you. You know how I told you that there's no Santa Claus?"

I froze and looked over at Ellery. Her eyes widened and she shook her head.

"Yes, princess. I remember."

"I changed my mind. I do believe in Santa Claus and I know he'll bring that girl at the coffee shop and her mom something really great for Christmas."

"That's great. What made you change your mind?" I asked.

"Me and Uncle Mason had a long talk last night and he told me all kinds of things about Santa Claus and then we watched a documentary on him."

I smiled as I stared at Ellery. "That's wonderful, Julia. We'll be home in a while and you can tell me all about it."

"Bye, Daddy. See you soon." *Click.*

I set the phone down on the table and Ellery narrowed her eyes at me.

"Julia told you that she didn't believe in Santa Claus and you didn't tell me?"

"I didn't want to upset you and she promised she wouldn't say anything to Collin."

"Oh yeah, because it's safe to trust the word of a seven-year-old."

"Baby, listen to me. She believes again, thanks to Mason. Now come here and sit on my lap."

She wrapped her arms around me and smiled as I kissed her lips. "One week until Christmas and, if you're a good girl, Santa may bring you lots of presents."

"So that means I can't be naughty, then." She smiled.

"You can be as naughty as you want to be with me. There are exceptions."

"I like exceptions," she said as she nipped my bottom lip.

Needless to say, we were a little late getting home.

As soon as we arrived back at the penthouse, we gave our children plenty of hugs and kisses and then Julia and Ellery went upstairs. Collin came with me to my office.

"Are you excited about Christmas?" I asked.

"Yeah," Collin replied as he zoomed his fire truck across the floor.

I smiled as I sat down at my desk and opened up the drawer.

"Oh shit!" I exclaimed as I pulled out the tickets I had bought for *The Nutcracker*, which was tonight.

"Daddy, you said a bad word."

"Sorry, Collin. Don't tell your mom."

He giggled.

"Come on, Collin. We need to talk to Mommy," I said as I grabbed his hand.

We walked upstairs and into the bedroom, where Ellery was unpacking our bag from last night.

"I have a surprise for you."

"I love surprises, Daddy." Julia smiled.

Ellery turned around and looked at me. "What kind of surprise?"

"We are going to see *The Nutcracker* ballet tonight." I smiled.

Julia put her little hands over her mouth and screamed. "Oh my God, Daddy! I'm so excited."

"Tonight, Connor?" Ellery asked.

I held up the four tickets I had in my hand. "Yeah. I sort of forgot it was tonight."

"Connor!"

"I know, baby. I'm sorry. With the holidays and the party and shopping, I forgot."

"Daddy said 'shit,'" Collin blurted out.

"Connor!"

"Thanks, buddy."

He giggled.

"So here's the plan. Dinner first, then *The Nutcracker.* So I suggest everyone starts getting ready right now."

"Mommy, can I wear my Christmas dress?" Julia excitedly asked.

"Yes. Go get changed and then I'll do your hair. Take your brother to his room and I'll be there in a minute."

The two of them walked out of the room and Ellery stood there with her arms folded, tapping her foot.

"I know you were planning on doing nothing but spending a quiet evening at home, but this will be fun. You saw how excited Julia was."

"You're right. It will be fun. I just wish you would have told me earlier; like when you first bought the tickets."

I walked over to her and clutched her hips. "I love you, Mrs. Black and I'm sorry."

"I love you too, Mr. Black. Now I think I'll put on the dress from last night." She smiled.

"I don't think so. Remember, you spilled salad dressing on it."

"Damn." She winked.

I called in reservations for pre-theater dining. It was times like these when being one of the most influential men in New York City came in handy. They were fully booked until I told them who I was. Immediately, they had a corner table available for my family. I knew the kids wouldn't like the food on the menu, so I put in a special request for chicken fingers and French fries. They were more than happy to accommodate us.

Ellery put herself together in record time and did Julia's hair. I helped get Collin ready and Denny arrived to drive us.

"How do I look, Daddy?" Julia asked as she spun around.

"Like a true princess." I smiled.

Ellery kissed my cheek as we stepped onto the elevator.

"What's that for?" I asked.

"For tonight."

I smiled as I took hold of her hand.

We had dinner first and the kids were happy with their chicken fingers. All Julia talked about was how she couldn't wait to see the beautiful girls on stage dance in their pretty ballet costumes. When we arrived at the theater, and before heading to our seats, Julia spotted the gift shop.

"Daddy, the gift shop. Let's go!" she said as she grabbed my hand and pulled me. She walked over to where the tiaras were. I thought she was going to explode.

"Look at how beautiful this is." She smiled as she picked up a tiara. "I want this."

"But Christmas is coming, princess."

"I don't care. I'm a princess and I need this tiara."

Ellery looked at me and smiled. "Way to go, Daddy."

"There's no harm in buying it. After all, we are at the ballet. The kids should have souvenirs."

Collin pointed to a nutcracker and said he wanted it. "See; he wants a nutcracker, she wants a tiara, and what do you want?" I smiled.

"I'm good, Connor."

I took the tiara from Julia and the nutcracker from Collin and took it up to the register. Once we were seated, I put the tiara on Julia's head.

"I officially crown you my princess." I smiled as I tapped her on the nose. Ellery looked at me and rolled her eyes, and I couldn't help but chuckle.

The Nutcracker was just as amazing as the first ten times I saw it. Julia loved it and Collin fell asleep. We had a wonderful family night without any meltdowns and I couldn't have been happier.

CHAPTER ELEVEN

Ellery

Connor left for the office and Mason came by to take Collin for the day while Julia and I went out. Our first stop was going to be to the coffee shop. We walked through the door and stood in the long line.

"Mommy, there's that girl. I'm going to sit with her. Okay?"

"Okay, Julia. Stay where I can see you."

I watched her as she went and sat down across from the young girl. When I approached the counter, the young woman greeted me with a warm smile.

"Is that your little girl sitting at the table?" I asked.

"Yes," she replied hesitantly.

"I'm sorry. It's just my daughter, Julia, is sitting over there with her and I was wondering if it's okay if I buy her a hot chocolate. I'm Ellery Black."

"Hi, I'm Jamie. She was in here the other day with—"

"Her brother and their nanny," I replied.

"Yes, that's right. Lexi was saying how nice she was."

"I'll have a medium latte with soy and two hot chocolates."

"Coming right up." She smiled.

"Thank you." I took my coffee and the two hot chocolates over to the table where the girls were sitting.

"One for you, Julia, and one for your friend." I smiled.

"Thank you, Mommy. This is Lexi."

"It's very nice to meet you, Lexi."

"It's nice to meet you too, Julia's mom."

As I took a seat at the table next to the girls, Jamie came and sat down across from me.

"That was very nice of you to get Lexi hot chocolate. Thank you again."

"Oh, please don't mention it. It's no big deal. Does she come her with you regularly?" I asked.

Jamie looked down and I could tell she was very hesitant to answer my question.

"My mom usually looks after her, but she had to go to Wisconsin to help my sister with her new baby and, with the holidays, I really can't afford a babysitter for the day."

"Mommy, can Lexi come and spend the day with us?" Julia asked.

"I think that's a good idea." I smiled.

"No. I'm sorry, but I can't allow that."

"Mom, please," Lexi begged.

"No, Lexi," she said firmly.

"I don't blame you. You don't know me. So I can understand your feelings."

Suddenly, Julia looked at Jamie. "Her name is Ellery Black and my father is Connor Black. He owns Black Enterprises and he has a lot of money. We live in a penthouse with an elevator and I have a nanny named Mason who sometimes looks after me and my little brother Collin. My mommy paints pretty pictures for her art gallery and she volunteers regularly at the soup kitchen. Sometimes, she makes us all go and help. She takes very good care of us, including my daddy, so you don't have to worry about Lexi. She'll be in good hands and, if you don't believe me, you can Google my dad."

"Wow." Jamie smiled. "Thank you, Julia."

"You're welcome."

Jamie looked at me and laughed. "How old is she again?"

"I don't even know anymore. I would love to take Lexi for the day. She and Julia could play together and it would be better than her sitting in here all day."

"I just couldn't impose like that."

"It's not imposing. I'm offering to help you out. I'll give you whatever you need. Driver's license, social security number, passport." I laughed.

"Thank you, Ellery, but I think just your phone number would be fine."

"You got it." We exchanged phone numbers and as soon as the girls finished their hot chocolate and we were getting ready to leave, the manager asked Jamie if she could work until eight o'clock because one of the others girls had just called in.

"I can't," she said.

I placed my hand on her arm. "Go ahead. Lexi will be fine. She can have dinner with us and, when you get home, call me and we'll bring her home."

"I do need the overtime," she said. "Thank you, Ellery. I don't know what to say."

"Nothing. Just do what you have to do and don't worry. You have my number, so call me when you feel like you want to check in."

She gave Lexi a hug and helped her with her coat. "Now you be a good girl for Mrs. Black and have fun playing with Julia."

"I will, Mom. Thanks."

I could see the excitement in Lexi's eyes because she wasn't going to be stuck at the coffee shop all day. I took both girls by the hand, walked out of the coffee shop, and met Denny down the street.

"Hello, ladies," Denny said. "Did you adopt a kid, Elle?"

"She's Julia's friend. Can you please take us to Black Enterprises?"

"Sure thing," he said as he closed the door.

We stepped off the elevator and headed towards Connor's office. Valerie wasn't at her desk, so I knocked lightly because I didn't know if he was in a meeting.

"Come in," he said.

"Daddy!" Julia exclaimed as she ran to him.

"Julia, Ellery. What a nice surprise."

"Daddy, this is my friend, Lexi. She's the girl from the coffee shop. She's going to spend the day with us."

"That's wonderful, princess. It's very nice to meet you, Lexi." Connor smiled as he shook her little hand.

He walked over to me and placed his hands on my hips and gave me a kiss on the lips. "What have you done?" he whispered. "Did you kidnap her or something?"

I lightly smacked him. "No. Of course not. Her mom, Jamie, and I just got to talking and Julia asked if she could spend the day with us."

"And her mother just let her go with you?"

"Yeah, after your daughter gave her the rundown on our family." I laughed. "Julia even told her to Google you."

"Smart girl," he said as he kissed my forehead.

"I'm going to take them shopping for a while, out to lunch, and then we'll head home. Jamie's manager asked her if she could work until eight because of a call in and I told her to do it and that we'll drop Lexi off at home later."

"Sounds good, baby. I'll see you later."

"Bye, Daddy." Julia smiled and waved.

We left the building and climbed into the limo. The next thing Lexi said broke my heart.

"I wish I had a daddy."

CHAPTER TWELVE

Connor

As soon as I stepped off the elevator, I could hear the laughter of two little girls and music coming from the living room.

"What's going on in there?" I asked as I walked into the kitchen and kissed Ellery.

"The girls are dancing around."

"Are you making homemade macaroni and cheese?"

"I sure am. It'll be ready in a few minutes."

I walked over to the aluminum pan that was covered with foil and lifted it up. "Is that fried chicken?"

"Yes. Mason made it. He just left a little while ago."

"Where's Collin?" I asked.

"Upstairs playing video games in his room."

I walked over to the fridge and pulled out a bottle of water. "Did you find out anything about Lexi?"

"She said she wished she had a daddy and when I asked her what happened to her dad, she told me that she never met him."

"That's sad. Poor kid."

Ellery had asked me to go get Collin for dinner while she went and told the girls. As I sat at the table and watched all three kids eating, an overwhelming feeling came over me about wanting another baby. Ellery must have known it by the look on my face because when I looked over at her, she was staring at me.

"Get it out of your head, Black. The answer is no."

I gave her my cocky smile. "I have no idea what you're talking about."

"Yes, you do."

"You don't even feel the littlest—"

"No," she interrupted. "It's the season, babe. The feeling will pass."

After we all finished our dinner, the girls went back to the living room and Collin followed behind. As I helped Ellery clean up the kitchen, her phone rang.

"That was Jamie, Lexi's mom. She just left work and said that she's coming to pick up Lexi. I told her that we'd bring her home, but she insisted."

"Okay," I said as I walked over to her and wrapped my arms around her waist. "Are you sure you don't want—"

"I'm positive," she interrupted again.

"Why don't you ever let me finish what I want to say?"

"Because you don't need to. I already can read your mind and I say no." She smiled as she kissed my lips.

I sighed as I walked into the living room. "Lexi, your mom is on her way to pick you up."

"Oh, I thought you were driving me home."

"We were going to, but your mom said no and that she'd come here."

"Probably because she doesn't want you to see our tiny apartment. She's embarrassed."

"Why would she be embarrassed?" Julia asked.

"Because it's really small and the heat isn't working right now."

"Why isn't your heat working?" I asked her.

"I don't know. Mommy keeps calling the maintenance guy, but he won't come over to fix it. Sometimes at night, it gets so cold that my mom lies in bed with me and wraps her body around me to keep me warm."

Ellery walked up behind me and clasped my shoulders. "You need to do something," she whispered.

"I will make some calls first thing tomorrow morning."

The elevator doors opened and Jamie stepped into the foyer. Ellery went to greet her while I went and got Lexi her coat from the closet.

"Mommy, look at what Mrs. Black bought me today." Lexi smiled as she opened the large bag with a few toys in it.

"That was very nice of her. Did you say thank you?"

"Yes."

"Jamie, this is my husband, Connor."

"It's nice to meet you," she said as she held out her hand. "Ellery, can I talk to you for a moment in private?"

"Sure," Ellery said as they walked to the kitchen and I followed behind.

"Thank you for looking after Lexi today, but I can't let her keep those things you bought her."

"Why?" Ellery asked.

"Because it's not right."

"It's Christmas and this is what our family does."

"We aren't a charity case."

"Nobody said you were and this isn't about charity, Jamie. We were out shopping and I bought Lexi a few things. I did the same for Julia and Collin," Ellery said.

"Lexi told Julia that she isn't getting anything for Christmas because you can't afford it," I said.

"Connor!" Ellery snapped.

Jamie looked down and took a seat at the table, and I took a seat across from her.

"Listen, I'm sorry, but you know how little girls are. They tell people everything. It's nothing to be ashamed of. Times are really tough right now."

She began to cry. "Do you know what it's like to have to work so hard and so much just to be able to put food on the table for your kid? Do you know what it's like to have to tell your child that she won't be getting anything for Christmas because I have to pay the rent? And then to top it off, the dirt bag maintenance man won't even come and fix the heat."

Ellery walked over and set a cup of tea down and put her arm around her. "I've seen a lot throughout my life and I've been through a lot. I've been volunteering at the homeless shelter for years. What about Lexi's father?"

"He left when he found out I was pregnant. He said that he couldn't be a father because his own life was out of control. Last

I heard, he was married and had another kid. Real nice guy, huh?"

"Why don't you go after him for some type of support?" I asked.

"Because I want to protect my daughter from him. She doesn't need to know what a loser he is and how he didn't want her. I'm doing the best I can and sometimes I just feel like I'm nothing but a failure."

My heart ached for this woman and her child. Ellery looked at me with tears in her eyes.

"I'm sorry. I'm so sorry for dumping all this on you. I'm going to get Lexi and leave. I'm so embarrassed."

As she began to get up, I placed my hand on hers. "Sit down and finish your tea first. There's nothing to be embarrassed of. You're a great mom who, from what I can see, is raising a beautiful and smart girl. You have some unfortunate circumstances and, sometimes, it's okay to ask for help when you need it."

"Thank you, Connor and Ellery, but Lexi and I will be fine."

"I know you will." I smiled as I got up and walked to my office. I walked back into the kitchen and placed a check in Jamie's hand. "You are not to deny this."

She looked at the check and then at me with widened eyes. "No. I won't."

"Every year, my company gives to a family in need with one stipulation – the family has to pay it forward. You are the family I want to give to this year. Go and buy your little girl something for Christmas and make sure to buy yourself something nice as well. I have a feeling it's been a long time since you've done something for yourself. It's okay to accept help. There's no shame in it at all and there's no shame in wanting to help people. The only thing I ask is that you pay it forward and help someone else out that is in need."

Tears poured from her eyes as she looked at the check and she shook her head. "You are kind and generous people. Thank you and I will pay it forward. I promise."

57

After I arrived at Black Enterprises, I made a few phone calls regarding the apartment building that Jamie and Lexi lived in. When I found out a few things, I decided to pay the owner a little visit.

"How can I help you?" Mr. Greggs said as he bit into a rather large sandwich.

"I've been hearing that you're not providing heat to your tenants."

"Where'd you hear that?"

"I heard it and that's all you need to know."

"Money's a little tight right now."

"That wouldn't have anything to do with your little gambling problem, would it?"

"Who the fuck are you? Get out of my office."

I put my hands in my coat pocket and cocked my head. "I'm the guy who's going to ruin your already pathetic life if you don't get this place up to code and get these people some heat. Have you ever been to jail, Mr. Greggs? Because from where I'm standing, it looks like it could be in your future."

"Are you threatening me?"

"Yes. I am threatening you and, if you're not careful, I'll come in and buy this building right out from under you. Considering the back taxes you owe and how out of code this building is, you'll owe me money. Am I making myself clear?"

He nodded his head as he sat back down in his chair.

"Good. You have until eight o'clock tonight to get the heat working in this building. Have a Merry Christmas, Mr. Greggs." I smiled as I walked out.

Later that evening, I gave Jamie a call to find out if her heat was working. She told me that it was and asked if I had anything to do with it. I simply told her that there would be a lot of changes that would be made to her building.

CHAPTER THIRTEEN

Ellery

Christmas Eve. I couldn't believe it was finally here, and in two more days, I'd be leaving on a week-long kid-free trip with my husband.

Julia, Collin, and I spent the last couple of days making Christmas cookies and Mason helped them build a gingerbread house. All the presents were wrapped and everything was all set for our celebration tonight with our closest friends.

"I can't wait for Santa Claus to come tonight!" Julia said with excitement.

"Yay!" Collin jumped up and down.

They were beaming with excitement. "Julia, why don't you take your brother and go watch a Christmas cartoon?"

"Okay, Mommy." She smiled.

I heard the elevator door open and Connor walked in. "Are you going to tell me where you went?" I smiled as I took off his scarf.

"No. You'll find out soon enough."

I took hold of his hands. "Your hands are cold," I said as I brought them up to my lips and kissed them softly.

"It's not going to work, baby. I'm not telling you anything."

I frowned as I let go of his hands. "Fine. I can wait."

I heard him chuckle as I walked away. As I poured a glass of wine, the caterers arrived. That was my cue to get out of the kitchen. When I walked into the living room, I found Julia and Collin asleep with Connor on the couch. I quietly went and got my phone, snapped a picture of them, and sent it to Peyton.

"Same thing over here. It must be all the excitement of Christmas," she replied as she sent me a picture of Henry and Hailey sleeping on the couch.

The elevator doors opened and Mason and Landon walked in.

"Shh," I whispered as I pointed.

"Do you want me to take them upstairs to their room? I can start with sexy daddy." Mason winked.

Just as I smacked him on the arm, Connor opened one eye.

"I heard that."

"Uncle Mason. Uncle Landon!" both kids exclaimed.

They jumped off of Connor and ran right into the arms of Mason and Landon. Connor got up from the couch and wished them a Merry Christmas as they lightly hugged.

"If you'll excuse me, I'm going upstairs to get ready. Julia, go put on your dress. Mason, can you help Collin get dressed? I've laid his clothes out on his bed."

"Of course. Come on, my prince. Let's get you all royal-like."

Landon laughed as he and Connor walked over to the bar. I went upstairs and pulled out the new silvery dress I had bought. As I was in the bathroom curling my hair, Connor walked in and his tongue trailed down my neck.

"I can't wait for tonight. I saved the best outfit for last and it may just contain some accessories."

"You're a very kinky man, Mr. Black. I hope I don't drink too much and pass out before we can have some fun."

"If you do, I'll still have my way with you. It'll just be unfortunate for you that you won't remember." He winked.

"Very funny. You need to get changed; people will be arriving soon."

He forcefully kissed me on the lips and smiled. "I love you."

"I love you too."

After finishing my hair and makeup, I slipped into my dress and then went downstairs to check on the caterers. Everything looked in order. The appetizers were sorted neatly on silver Christmas platters. Champagne and wine were poured in beautiful holiday glasses and dinner smelled delicious. As I grabbed a glass of champagne, Connor walked up from behind and wrapped his warm arms around me.

"You look beautiful."

"Thank you, my love. Are you ready to entertain?"

"I'm always ready." He winked.

All of our guests had arrived and Connor and I walked around and entertained.

"So, does Connor suspect anything about his gift yet?" Peyton asked.

"No. And he hasn't even mentioned anything."

"What about for you? What did he get you?"

"I don't know. It's weird because, usually, he's hounding me about telling him what I want. He only asked one time and that was in Tiffany's. Other than that, he hasn't asked me at all, so I'm not sure what he has up his sleeve."

"Maybe he bought you another art gallery." She laughed.

"You know, I wouldn't mind one in Paris."

"I wouldn't put it past him. You know if you asked for one, he'd buy it for you."

Dinner was ready and being served, so I went and found Collin while Connor told Julia to get to the table. He sat at the head of the table and made a toast.

"Thank you for coming this evening and celebrating Christmas with our family. Each and every one of you that is here with us is very special and an important part of our lives and we couldn't imagine celebrating this holiday without you. To my beautiful wife, Ellery. I fall more and more in love with you every single day."

A tear sprang to my eye as I held up my glass. Suddenly, in a room full of silence, Julia cleared her throat.

"Ahem. Go on, Daddy."

"To my beautiful princess, Julia. You are growing so fast and, before we know it, you'll be a teenager driving us crazy and then you'll be thirty years old and still living with us." He smiled.

"Daddy!" She giggled.

"To my son, Collin, my little boy who is already growing up so fast. Before we know it, he'll be standing here, making a toast to his family one day."

"Why does he get to have a family and I don't?" Julia pouted.

"Because your daddy's crazy," Denny whispered as he reached over and tickled her. She giggled.

We all enjoyed a wonderful dinner and dessert, and then it was time to gather by the fire and open presents. Once we finished, Connor sat in his chair and read *T'was the Night before Christmas*, like he did every year. It was a wonderful night and, as soon as the last guest left, Connor took a very sleepy Collin upstairs and helped him change into his pajamas.

"Come on, Julia. It's time for bed. Santa Claus won't come if you're not sleeping."

"Okay, Mommy. I'm so excited! I can't wait until tomorrow."

As soon as she was in her pajamas, I tucked her into bed and kissed her head.

"Mommy, why does Daddy keep saying that I have to live with you guys forever?"

I smiled as I sat down on the edge of the bed. "Your daddy has been saying that since you were first born. I remember when you were just a tiny baby, I walked in on a conversation your dad was having with you and he said that you were never allowed to date and that you'd live with us forever. But don't worry, baby. You're going to find the man of your dreams one day, get married, and start a family of your own. You don't pay any attention to your dad."

"I can hear you, Ellery."

"Oops. We got caught." I smiled at Julia.

Connor walked over and kissed her good night and then took my hand and led me out of the room. I walked over to Collin's room and gave him a kiss. We went downstairs, filled the children's stockings, and then it was off to our bedroom for a sinful night of Christmas sex.

CHAPTER FOURTEEN

Connor

"**M**ommy, Daddy!" Julia and Collin excitedly yelled as they ran into our room and jumped on the bed. "It's Christmas!"

I opened my eyes and looked at the clock. Good God; it was only six a.m. Ellery and I didn't finally get to sleep until two.

"Merry Christmas, Julia and Collin." I smiled as they climbed in between us.

Ellery rolled over and smiled. "Merry Christmas. You two go downstairs and we'll be down in a minute."

They jumped off the bed and ran out of the bedroom. I rolled over and wrapped my arms around Ellery as she snuggled tightly against me.

"Merry Christmas, baby."

"Merry Christmas, darling." She smiled as she kissed me. "We better get downstairs before they come back up and tackle us again."

We went downstairs and I told Ellery to go in the living room with the kids and I'd start the coffee. Last night was amazing and I was still thinking about it. The kids were sitting patiently in the middle of the floor, waiting to open their presents.

"Look; this one is from Santa Claus." I smiled as I handed Julia and Collin each a present.

Julia ripped it open as fast as she could and squealed when she saw it was an iPad. Collin squealed when he opened up the train set he wanted.

"I'll go pour us some coffee." Ellery smiled as she kissed me.

It didn't take the kids very long to open all the gifts we bought them. They were happy and got everything they wanted. Julia was happy with her Hello Kitty iPad case and immediately put her iPad in it.

"It's Mommy's turn to open her presents." I smiled.

"It's your turn, darling. I've been dying for this day for a while now and I can't wait."

"Me too, Elle. Let's open them together."

She handed me a small square box and I handed her one. We both opened them at the same time and I looked at her as I pulled out the gloves. She then handed me another box and I noticed that the presents were numbered, just like I had done for hers. When I opened the ski jacket and she opened hers, we looked at either in confusion.

"You didn't," we both said at the same time.

I decided to skip over a couple of the other gifts and give her the last one I had marked. She did the same. When I unwrapped the box and took off the lid, there were two airline tickets to Aspen, leaving tomorrow morning at seven o'clock.

"Ellery," I said as I looked at her. "Open yours."

She took off the wrapping and gasped when she saw the plane itinerary for Aspen and the confirmation reservation for the St. Regis.

"I can't believe you did all this." She smiled.

"Baby, I can't believe *you* did all this."

She sat there, shaking her head. "Wow. You bought everything for the ski trip. I can't believe we both thought of the same thing to get each other."

"We'd been talking about a trip for us for a long time and I couldn't think of anything better than to go skiing with you at Christmas time."

"Great taste in the ski jacket by the way," she said as she got up and pulled the same one out of the closet.

"I thought you'd look sexy as hell in that color." I winked.

She walked over to me and sat down on my lap, wrapping her arms around me and hugging me tight.

"I love you so much. Thank you for everything."

"I love you more, Ellery, and thank you for everything. It makes me so happy that you planned this trip, even though I planned the same one. We really are two of a kind. Aren't we?"

"We sure are." She smiled as we passionately kissed.

"Ew, stop it!" Julia said.

"That's gross," Collin followed.

We both laughed. "As much as I love our children, I can't wait to be alone with you for a week," I whispered as I pushed a strand of her hair back.

"So who did you get to watch them?" she asked.

"My parents."

She shook her head. "Me too. Damn, they are really good at keeping secrets."

"So which plane are we taking?" I asked her.

"Since I paid for the tickets already, I think we should fly commercial."

"Somehow, I knew you'd say that. The money isn't an issue, baby."

"I know it's not, but let's do things differently this time."

"Fine. We'll fly commercial, but we'll stay in the room I reserved."

"The Presidential Suite? Right?"

"Yes." I smiled.

"That's odd because I reserved that suite as well and I know they only have one."

"That is strange. Well, we'll see when we get there. Julia, Collin, play quietly with your toys. Mommy and Daddy are going upstairs to get ready to go to Grandma and Grandpa's," I said as I picked up Ellery and carried her.

"Why are you carrying Mommy?" Julia asked.

I stopped and turned around. "Because I love her and she's my queen."

"Oh," Julia said as she looked back down at her iPad.

Ellery brushed her lips against mine. I took her upstairs, locked the door, and began making passionate love to her until the knocks on the door started.

"I can't wait to leave tomorrow," I said.

"Me either." She smiled.

We loaded the kids and the presents in the Range Rover and headed over to my parents' house. We sat them down before we left and explained to them that they would be spending the week at Grandma's house because we were leaving for a trip tomorrow. They didn't seem to mind and said they were looking forward to spending the week with their grandparents. My mom was thrilled to have them and she had already planned all kinds of activities.

"Merry Christmas." My mom smiled as she greeted us at the door. "Come here, my little babies."

"I'm not a baby, Grandma. I'm seven."

"Of course, Julia."

"Mom, who called you first about Aspen?" I asked with a smile.

"You both called me on the same day, fifteen minutes apart. Connor, you called first and when Ellery called and told me that she had to call the St. Regis and hoped that the Presidential Suite was available, I called them immediately and explained to them what was going on."

"So that's why they didn't say anything when I booked the room." Ellery smirked.

We walked to the family room where the rest of the family was.

"Uncle Connor, Aunt Ellery," Camden said as he walked over and looked at us.

"Merry Christmas. Can I have a hug?" I asked.

"Just be careful not to squeeze too tight," he replied with seriousness.

I gave him a hug and Ellery did the same. "Her hugs are better," he said, and then walked out of the room.

"Merry Christmas, son," my dad said as we lightly hugged. "Merry Christmas, Elle. You look beautiful."

"Thanks, Dad. Merry Christmas." Ellery smiled.

I walked over to the bar and poured a glass of scotch for myself and a glass of wine for Ellery. As I handed it to her, I softly kissed her lips as I stared into her beautiful blue eyes. I couldn't stop thinking about our trip.

"They've been kissing like that all day," Julia said.

"Yeah. It's gross," Collin spewed.

Ellery and I laughed as we walked into the kitchen to see if my mom needed any help.

"How are you, big brother?" Cassidy asked as she hooked her arm around me.

"I'm good, sis." I smiled.

It was time for dinner and we all gathered around the table and said Grace before digging into my mother's wonderful holiday meal.

CHAPTER FIFTEEN

Ellery

Connor's dad called all the kids over by the fire and made them sit in a circle while he read them a Christmas story.

"He never did that when Cassidy and I were kids," Connor said.

"He's older now and those are his grandkids. I have a feeling you'll be doing the same with your grandkids."

"Hell, I do it now with my own kids." Connor smiled as he tapped me on the nose.

"I still can't believe we both booked the same trip."

"I still can't believe that you're making me fly commercial."

"You'll live. You have so far with the things I've made you do."

"True. But why didn't you just book the company plane?"

"Because then you would have known or I would have known. The pilot would have told one of us."

"Smart, Ellery."

"I know." I winked.

Connor and I stared at the kids as they sat next to their grandpa and listened intently as he read them a story.

"Thank you," Connor said as he kissed the side of my head.

"For what?"

"For giving me two beautiful children."

"If I recall, you had something to do with that too."

"I just gave you sperm. You did all the rest."

I laughed as he pulled me into him and hugged me.

It was getting late and Connor and I still had to pack for our trip, so we said our goodbyes. I knelt down to Collin and Julia.

"I want the both of you to be very good for Grandma and Grandpa. Okay?"

"Of course I will, Mommy. I can't really speak for Collin, since he's a baby."

"I am not a baby, Julia!" Collin yelled.

"Julia."

"Mommy." She smiled.

I kissed them both and stood up. "It's your fault," I said as I looked at Connor.

He sighed and knelt down in front of them. "Princess. Please stop calling your brother a baby and Collin, please stop yelling. You need to behave or Grandma and Grandpa won't watch you anymore."

"Of course they will, Daddy. Don't be silly," Julia said.

"Goodbye, my children. We will see you in a week," he said as he took hold of my hand and led me out to the Range Rover.

"What's wrong? Couldn't get out of there fast enough?" I laughed.

"Yes, and you know why?"

"Because your daughter is a diva?"

"No. Because the first place I'm fucking you when we get back to the penthouse is underneath the Christmas tree. I've been waiting to unwrap you all day and I've waited long enough. Brace yourself, baby. You're in for one hell of an unwrapping."

Connor

"Ah, the joys of flying commercial. Baggage check, security, lines galore."

"Connor, stop complaining. You'll be just fine," I said.

We finally made it through security and Ellery and I headed to our gate. Once we boarded, we took our seats in first class and were warmly greeted by a very pretty flight attendant who wouldn't stop staring at me.

"May I offer you something to drink?" she asked.

"I'll have a scotch. Thank you." I smiled.

"Isn't it a little early to be drinking, Connor?"

"Not for me." I smirked.

"And you, ma'am?"

"I'll have a cup of coffee with some Baileys, please."

"Isn't it a little early to be drinking, Ellery?"

"Not when I have to sit here and watch that bitch flirt with you for the next how many hours."

I chuckled as I brought her hand up to my lips.

I opened up my iPad and began reading the *Wall Street Journal.* Ellery opened hers and began reading a book.

"Are you sure you don't want another baby?" I asked out of the clear blue.

She glared at me. "I'm positive. Where is this coming from all of a sudden?"

I sighed. "I don't know. I guess it's because Julia and Collin are growing up so fast and, before you know it, there won't be any children in the house anymore."

"So you want to keep having kids because our other kids are growing up?"

"Something like that." I smiled.

"Connor, I love our family. I love you and our two children. Do you really want to go through all the postpartum, mood swings, sleepless nights, illnesses, crying nonstop?"

"Now that you mention all that. I'm happy with the way things are."

"I knew you just needed a gentle reminder. But to be honest, sometimes I do think about it."

"We're good, Elle. Our family of four is all I'll ever need."

The flight attendant stopped by again and asked me if I needed anything. I could tell Ellery was getting really pissed because the way the flight attendant was looking at me wasn't normal.

"Excuse me," Ellery said. "Can I have a blanket?"

"Sure."

"Make sure it's a big one that will cover both of us. I don't want the people across the way knowing that I'm giving my husband a hand job."

Her eyes widened as she looked at me. "I'm so sorry," I said to her.

Ellery busted out laughing. "She deserved it. Good God, Connor. I think if you would have gotten up to go to the bathroom, she would have raped you in there."

"Ellery. That's not funny."

"Yes it is, baby." She smiled as she kissed my lips.

"Please promise me you'll behave on this trip. Please, Elle."

"I'll do my best. But if any women try to mess with you, I'm stepping in."

I sighed. It was same thing every time we went out.

CHAPTER SIXTEEN

Two layovers later and more complaints about commercial flying from Connor, we finally landed in Aspen.

"You know I can't even look at that flight attendant."

"Good. You shouldn't be anyway."

"I wanted another drink."

"Then you should have told me and I would have gotten her attention." I smiled.

"You're crazy."

"You love my crazy."

We found our way to baggage claim and Connor grabbed our suitcases. I began to laugh my ass off when I saw two men holding up signs. One said *Mr. Connor Black* and the other said *Mrs. Connor Black.*

"Oops. I forgot to cancel the car service I rented us."

Connor looked at me and shook his head. "I'm sorry, but my wife and I both reserved cars without knowing the other did." I pulled out my wallet and gave the driver that Ellery reserved his fee. "I'm sorry, but take that for driving out here. We'll be taking this limo."

We climbed into the back and I looked at him. "What was wrong with the limo I rented for us? That driver was hot."

"Exactly. That's why I sent him on his way."

I rolled my eyes and smiled. "You're bad, Mr. Black."

"I just want you to know that you will pay for being bad on the airplane."

"Bring it on, Black. You don't scare me."

He chuckled as he softly kissed me.

After checking in at the St. Regis, the bellhop took our luggage up to the Presidential Suite. When we walked inside the room, I took in a deep breath and smiled. It was gorgeous.

"It's beautiful, Connor."

"It sure is, baby."

While Connor tipped the bellhop, I walked over to the window and stared out at the beautiful snow-capped mountains. Connor came up from behind and wrapped his arms around me.

"This makes me very happy; me and you."

"Me too. Are we bad parents?" I asked.

"No, Elle. We're wonderful parents who just need a little break from their children. I'm starving. Why don't we change and go to dinner."

"Good idea. I'm hungry too."

We changed and went downstairs to the restaurant in the hotel and had an amazing dinner by the fireplace. Once we were finished, we took a stroll outside and explored the grounds. The snow was lightly falling and I was in awe over the Christmas lights and trees that were elegantly decorated.

"Tomorrow, we'll ski and then we'll get massages," Connor said.

"I booked us snowboarding lessons for the next day," I said.

"I can't wait. I've always wanted to snowboard. It's just something I never did."

"It'll be fun. Just the two of us learning together. Now kiss me. My lips are cold." I smiled.

"Mrs. Black, your whole body is cold. I think we need to get you back up to the room and into a hot bath."

"Only if you promise to join me."

"I would never make you bathe alone." He winked.

As soon as we got back to the room, Connor flipped on the light switch. There sat a massive bouquet of pink roses on the table.

"Connor, look at how beautiful these are. They must be from the hotel."

"There's a card. What does it say?"

I took the card that was leaning up against the beautiful crystal vase and opened the envelope.

To the most beautiful woman in the world.

Infinity is forever, and that's what you are to me, Mrs. Black. You're my forever.

Love,

Connor

I closed my eyes as my heart began to pick up the pace. As I turned around, Connor immediately wiped the tears that fell from my eyes.

"Don't cry, baby."

"Thank you. You are my forever, Mr. Black, and I will love you for eternity. You're perfect to me in every way possible and you're perfect to our children. Thank you for loving us as much as you do."

"Ellery," he whispered as his lips softly met mine.

He picked me up and carried me to the bedroom and gently laid me down on the bed, where he made love to me as slowly and passionately as possible.

A couple of days had passed and we went skiing. I fell a few times and Connor laughed at me. I wasn't the best at skiing, but I tried. Connor was an amazing skier. The way he moved had me turned on ninety-nine percent of the time. We had a great time and, afterwards, we got a couples massage. I had a hot guy and he had a beautiful sexy woman. Needless to say, we both switched.

"Are you ready to go snowboarding?" Connor asked.

"I sure am. Just let me grab my jacket."

We headed down the mountain where our instructor was waiting for us. He first showed us how to properly strap our boots onto the board. Once he was confident and checked us, he began our lesson. Connor and I mostly goofed around for the first half of the lesson because the instructor wanted us to get the feel of it first. As we progressed throughout the day, and Connor fell a few times, we started to really snowboard. I didn't fall at all, which was weird, considering I couldn't ski well. The instructor had us start with a very small hill and Connor went first. He looked sexy as hell as he boarded down that hill and then stopped without any mishaps. Next, it was my turn and I wasn't so sure.

"What's wrong, Elle? Are you chicken? Are you afraid that you'll fall like you always do when you ski?"

That was it. He pissed me off! I took off down that hill and passed him up, keeping my balance as I moved my body from side to side. I stopped when I reached another small hill and saw Connor coming for me.

"You show off!" he said.

"Try to catch me, big shot!" I said as I took off down the hill.

He followed, and we were doing pretty well until I decided to stop and he ran into me, knocking us both down into the snow.

"Why did you stop like that? And how are you good at this?"

I laughed. "Sorry. I really didn't mean to stop, and I am good, aren't I?"

"You're amazing and so sexy when you snowboard. I'm hard, Ellery."

"Keep it in your pants, Black. I'll take care of you later. Right now, I'm ready to do some more snowboarding."

I got up and took off. I could hear Connor laugh as he did some small jumps. After about an hour, we decided to quit and go back to the hotel. It was cold and we were tired. Once we were in the room, Connor started the bathtub and climbed in. I undressed and twisted my hair up before climbing in and nestling myself between his legs. I laid my head back on his chest and looked up as his lips meet mine.

"I love you, Ellery."

"I love you, Connor. Today was so fun."

"It was very fun. Thank you for this wonderful Christmas gift."

"You're welcome. Thank you for this wonderful Christmas gift," I said as my fingers caressed his arms. "So far, this trip has been absolutely amazing, but I miss the kids, Connor."

"They're fine, Elle. They're having fun with my mom and dad. I'm sure they're not even giving us a second thought."

"You're probably right."

"I know I'm right, baby. Now turn around."

I smiled as I turned and wrapped my legs around his waist as he sat up. His tongue lingered across my neck and up to my earlobe. I could feel his cock getting harder by the second. I wanted him. I needed him, and I wasted no time taking him inside me.

I ordered room service so we could eat breakfast by the window and watch the snow fall.

"I booked you a facial for today at four o'clock."

"You did?" she asked.

"Yep."

"Are you saying that I need one?"

"No, Ellery. I'm saying that I know how much you love facials and I thought you'd like one."

"Okay. Sounds good. What are you going to do?"

"I don't know. Probably hang out at the bar and wait for you."

"Can we go shopping today?"

"How about if we do that tomorrow? I have another surprise for you."

"You're full of surprises, Mr. Black. I think I might love you." She smiled.

We finished breakfast and then I told Ellery to bundle up. When we walked outside of the hotel, our horse and carriage was waiting for us.

"Oh, Connor. No way."

"Yes way, baby."

The smile on her face was magical. We climbed in and took a ride through the trails of the mountains. Ellery snuggled against me as I wrapped us in a blanket. The scenery looked like it was something from a Hallmark card.

"This is gorgeous, Connor. Look at these trails, the snow, and the mountains. Have you ever seen anything more beautiful?"

"Actually, I have," I replied as I kissed her head.

She lifted her head and looked at me as she locked her lips with mine. We arrived back at the hotel in just enough time for Ellery to change and get down to the spa for her facial.

"I'll be in the bar. Just come there when you're done."

"I will." She smiled.

I took the last sip of my scotch when I saw Ellery walk in. She was glowing.

"Well, how did it go?"

"It was nice. Very relaxing. She said I had a natural glow to my face."

"It's from all the sex we constantly have." I smiled.

"That's what I was thinking. Can we call the kids?" she asked with a sad tone.

"I just tried a few minutes ago and there was no answer. My parents must have them out somewhere."

"Did you try your parents' cell phones?"

"Yep. No answer. We can try again after dinner. Let's go get ready."

"Can't I have a drink first?" Ellery asked as she sat on the stool.

"No. You can have a drink upstairs."

"Connor, what's wrong with you?"

"Nothing. I'm hungry, Elle."

"Fine. Let's go up to the room."

Once we entered the room, I poured Ellery some champagne and handed her the glass.

"Here's your drink, baby."

"I still don't know why I couldn't have one down at the bar."

I ignored her as I changed my shirt. There was knock on the door and I asked Ellery if she could get it while I went into the bathroom.

She opened the door and I smiled when I heard her gasp.

"Mommy!" Julia and Collin screamed.

"What. Oh my God. Wait. What," she said as she hugged them tightly.

I stood there with a smile on my face as they ran to me and I hugged them. Ellery had tears in her eyes as she hugged Mason and Landon. Then she turned and looked at me.

"You missed them and so did I. So I brought them to us."

"I have no words for you right now, Connor Black." She began to cry.

"Why is Mommy crying?" Julia asked.

"Because she's so happy to see you and Collin. We missed you both very much."

"We missed you too. Grandma and Grandpa are nice and all, but they aren't very fun."

Ellery began to laugh. She put her arms around both kids and led them over to the couch while she kept kissing their heads.

"Mom, stop!" Collin said.

"No. I missed you and I'm so happy you're here."

"So, sexy daddy. Do we get you to see you moving those hips on a snowboard?" Mason asked.

"Do you know how to snowboard?" I asked.

"No. How hard can it be?"

Ellery looked at me and bit down on her bottom lip while I put my arm around Mason. "We'll go tomorrow."

"I can't wait. If you need us, we'll be down the hall."

"Okay, Black family. Who's hungry? I know I am and I want food."

"I am," Julia and Collin both said.

We took the kids out for a nice dinner and, when we came back, they were tired and ready for bed. I helped Collin into his pajamas, while Ellery brushed Julia's hair. The suite had two bedrooms, so Ellery and I could still be alone and be intimate. Except this time, we had to be very quiet. We tucked them each into their own queen-sized beds and kissed them goodnight. Ellery stood there and looked at them from the doorway.

"Baby, what are you doing?" I asked.

"Watching my babies sleep. I can't believe they're here. As much as I love you and love spending time alone with you, I missed them so much."

"I did too, Elle. It just felt weird without them. Now, my thinking is that they're still very young and that's why we're feeling this way. But when they get to be teenagers, I have a feeling we'll be sneaking away a lot."

"I think you're right." She smiled as she kissed me. This was a magical and wonderful Christmas, Connor, and it's one I'll never forget."

"I'll never forget it either, Ellery. We are so lucky to have what we do and I wouldn't trade any of it for anything in the world. You and my children are the best part of me and all three of you make the world a better place."

She stood there with tears in her eyes and I gently wiped them away. "Since the kids are asleep, why don't we have Mason and Landon come stay with them and we can go down to the bar and have that drink."

"I would love that, Mr. Black."

Ellery

We rang in the New Year with a bang and then took the plane back home on New Year's Day. It felt so good to be back home. Don't get me wrong; I loved every second of Aspen, but I missed my and Connor's bed as well as the comfort of all of our things. As we unpacked and got settled, Connor ordered us Chinese food and the four of us started to take the ornaments off the tree and carefully pack them away until next year.

"Do you think we could go to Disneyland next year?" Julia asked.

"Sure; why not?" Connor replied.

"Thanks, Daddy. I'm holding you to it."

I laughed.

"Oh, and by the way, I'm bored with my Hello Kitty case. I saw a way cooler one online and I would like you to order it, please."

Connor looked at me and then at her. "Sorry, princess. You're not getting another iPad case. That's the one you wanted and that's the one you're keeping."

"We'll see, Daddy." She smiled.

"Your fault," I mouthed to him.

He laughed as we continued taking the ornaments off the tree. We were a tight-knit family and Connor made sure that we did everything together, even the smallest things. Next, we would celebrate Easter, birthdays, Fourth of July, Thanksgiving, and then Christmas again. Every year, we would build traditions and memories for our children to hold onto. Before Connor and I would know it, they'd be grown and married with families of their own. That day would come soon enough. But for now, the memories we were building with them would be for life, and they'd be memories they would treasure forever.

The End

About the Author

Sandi Lynn is a New York Times, USA Today and Wall Street Journal bestselling author who spends all of her days writing. She published her first novel, Forever Black, in February 2013. Her addictions are shopping, romance novels, coffee, chocolate, margaritas, and giving readers an escape to another world.

Please come connect with her at:
www.facebook.com/Sandi.Lynn.Author
www.twitter.com/SandilynnWriter
www.authorsandilynn.com
www.pinterest.com/sandilynnWriter
www.instagram.com/sandilynnauthor
https://www.goodreads.com/author/show/6089757.Sandi_Lynn

Printed in Great Britain
by Amazon